HORRID HENRY'S
Krazy Ketchup

Francesca Simon spent her childhood on the beach
in California, and then went to Yale and Oxford
Universities to study medieval history and literature.
She now lives in London with her family. She has
written more than 50 books and won the Children's
Book of the Year in 2008 at the Galaxy British Book
Awards for *Horrid Henry and the Abominable Snowman*.

There is a complete list of **Horrid Henry**
titles including picture books, Early Readers, joke
books and gift books at the end of the book.

Visit Horrid Henry's website at
www.horridhenry.co.uk for competitions,
games, downloads and a monthly newsletter!

HORRID HENRY'S
Krazy Ketchup

Francesca Simon
Illustrated by Tony Ross

Orion
Children's Books

First published in Great Britain in 2014
by Orion Children's Books
a division of the Orion Publishing Group Ltd
Orion House
5 Upper Saint Martin's Lane
London WC2H 9EA
An Hachette UK Company

7 9 10 8 6

Text © Francesca Simon 2014
Illustrations © Tony Ross 2014

The moral right of Francesca Simon and Tony Ross
to be identified as author and illustrator of this
work has been asserted.

All rights reserved. No part of this publication may be
reproduced, stored in a retrieval system, or transmitted,
in any form or by any means, electronic, mechanical,
photocopying, recording or otherwise, without the prior
permission of Orion Children's Books.

The Orion Publishing Group's policy is to use papers that
are natural, renewable and recyclable products and made
from wood grown in sustainable forests. The logging and
manufacturing processes are expected to conform to the
environmental regulations of the country of origin.

A catalogue record for this book is
available from the British Library.

Printed in Great Britain by
Clays Ltd, St Ives plc

ISBN 978 1 4440 0017 7

To David Abell and Seann Alderking,
the loveliest of lovely friends,
and all our good times together

CONTENTS

HORRID HENRY AND THE REVENGE OF THE BOGEY BABYSITTER

"I challenge you to a name-calling competition," shrieked Rude Ralph. "For the title of champion name-caller of the universe."

Ha, thought Horrid Henry. No one knew more rude names than Henry. Not even Rude Ralph.

"You're on," said Horrid Henry. "Woofy."

"Pongy."

"Smelly."

"Whiffy."

"Stinky."

"Reeky."

"Farty."

"Umm . . . Ummm . . ."
said Ralph.

"Umm isn't a name,"
crowed Henry. "Nah
Na Ne Nah Nah, I am
champion."

"Shut up, I'm
thinking," said
Ralph. "Poo
breath."

"Gloppy
Goop."

"Smellovision."

"Odiferous."

"Odiferous?

2

That's not a word,"
said Ralph.

"Is too."

"Is not."

"Wibble pants."

"Barf breath."

"Turkey head."

"Turkey head?" said
Rude Ralph. "*Turkey
head*? That's not a—"

Ding Dong.

Horrid Henry
stopped jumping up
and down on Ralph's
bed.

"Who's that?" said
Henry.

Ralph shrugged.

"We're having a babysitter
tonight," he said.

3

Horrid Henry's eyes gleamed.

A babysitter! Yeah. What could be better than a sleepover at Ralph's with a babysitter? He'd yet to meet one he couldn't tame. After all, he wasn't called the Bulldozer of Babysitters for nothing. A sitter meant hours of rampaging fun. Especially as Ralph was bound to have one of those brilliant babysitters who let you stay up all night and eat biscuits till you were sick and watch scary movies on TV. The kind his mean, horrible parents *never* ever got for him.

"Great," said Henry. "Who?" He hoped it would be Leafy Leon. He just sat with his headphones on doing his homework. Or Allergic Alice, who he'd heard was always too busy sneezing to see kids sneaking sweets. Or maybe – oh please please please – Dippy Dora. Margaret said Dora had spent the whole

4

evening on her phone and hadn't even noticed when Margaret stayed up past midnight and ate all the ice cream in the freezer.

"Dunno," said Ralph. "Mum didn't say. Probably Dora."

Yes! thought Horrid Henry.

"And Mum's baked a chocolate fudge cake," said Ralph.

"All for us?" said Henry.

"Nah," said Ralph. "Just a slice each."

Ralph looked at Henry.

Henry looked at Ralph.

"You thinking what I'm thinking?" said Henry.

"Oh yeah," said Ralph.

They could guzzle the *whole* cake and blame it on the babysitter. What brilliant luck,

thought Horrid Henry. Hmm boy,
he could taste that yummy, gooey
scrumptious chocolate cake already.

Stomp.
   Stomp.
      Stomp.

There was the sound of elephants
trampling.

"What was that?" said Horrid Henry.

Boom.
   Boom.
      Boom.

The elephants were joined by a herd of stampeding rhinoceroses.

"You don't think—" whispered Henry.

"It can't be . . ." whispered Ralph.

The walls shook.

Henry gasped.

The ground shook.

Ralph gulped.

"We'd better go and see," said Rude Ralph.

Henry and Ralph crept down the stairs and peeked round the door.

AAARRRGHHHHHH!

Stomping towards them was the biggest, meanest, ugliest, hideously horrible teen Henry remembered from his worst nightmares. Enormous kid-mashing arms: check. Enormous spiky head: check. Enormous Henry-hating eyes and child-chewing fangs: check.

It was Rabid Rebecca, the bogey babysitter, risen from the swamp where she thrashed around with the Loch Ness Monster and the Creature from the Black Lagoon.

"When you said you were having a babysitter, you never said it could be – Rebecca," hissed Horrid Henry.

"I didn't know," whimpered Rude Ralph.

"We're doomed," moaned Horrid Henry.

"Where's the food?" bellowed Rabid Rebecca.

Ralph's mum pointed to the kitchen. "The boys can have a small slice of cake each," she trilled. "Be good," she shouted over her shoulder as she escaped.

Then Rebecca saw Henry.

Henry saw Rebecca.

"You," said Rabid Rebecca. Her evil eyes narrowed.

"Me," said Horrid Henry.

Last time he'd met Rabid Rebecca they'd had a fight almost to the death. Henry had hoped never to have a re-match. Then he remembered her weakness . . .

"Don't worry, she's scared of spiders," whispered Henry. "All we have to do is find some—"

"And don't get any ideas about spiders," said Rebecca. "I brought my friend Rachel. Nothing scares *her*."

10

Horrid Henry gasped as a terrifying fiend cast a black shadow over the sitting room.
Rancid Rachel was *even* tougher looking than Rabid Rebecca.

Rancid Rachel glared at Henry and Ralph. Her fangs gleamed.

"If I were you, I'd get straight upstairs to bed," growled Rachel. "That way I won't step on you by mistake."

"But what about my chocolate cake?" squeaked Ralph.

11

"My mum said—"

"*Our* cake, you mean," said the bogey babysitters.

"Don't you touch that cake!" squeaked Ralph.

"Yeah," said Horrid Henry. "Or else."

Rancid Rachel cracked her knuckles.

"Or else what?" she snarled.

Horrid Henry took a step back.

"Ooh, doesn't that cake look yummy," said Rachel. "Doncha think, Becs?"

"Yeah," said Rabid Rebecca. "I can't wait to eat it. Nice of the brat's mum to leave it all for us. Now go to bed before we EAT . . . YOU!"

"I'm not moving," said Horrid Henry.

"Yeah," said Rude Ralph. "Make me."

"GET OUT OF HERE!" boomed the bogey babysitters, exhaling their dragon breath.

Horrid Henry and Rude Ralph sat in his bedroom. They could hear the bogey babysitters cackling and laughing in the kitchen below.

"We've *got* to stop them stealing all the cake," said Ralph. "It's not fair."

"I know," said Henry.

13

"But how?" said Ralph. "She told us to stay in bed."

"So what," said Horrid Henry. He scowled. There had to be *something* they could do to stop the crime of the century.

"How?" said Ralph. "Call the police?"

Tempting, thought Horrid Henry. But somehow he didn't think the police would be too keen to race over and arrest two horrible babysitters for scoffing a cake.

"We could tell Rebecca it's poisoned," said Ralph.

"What, your mum made you a poisoned cake?" said Henry. "Don't think they'd believe you."

Rude Ralph hung his head.

14

"It's hopeless," said Ralph. "Now we won't get any."

No cake? No yummy chocolate cake dripping with fudgy frosting and studded with sweets?

Horrid Henry wasn't the Squisher of Sitters for nothing. Wasn't there some film he'd seen, or story he'd heard, where . . . where . . .

"Get some keys and some string," said Henry. "And one of your dad's suits on a hanger. Hurry."

"Why?" said Ralph.

"Do you want that cake or don't you?" said Henry. "Now do exactly what I say."

"AAAAARRGGGHHHH!"

The blood-curdling scream echoed through the house.

AAAAAARRRGGGGHHHHHHH!

AAAAAARRRGGGGHHHHHHH!
AAAAAARRRGGGGHHHHHHH!

Trudge.
Trudge.
Trudge.

Rabid Rebecca flung open Ralph's bedroom door. She glared at them screaming and trembling in the corner and flashed her child-chewing fangs.

"Stop screaming, you little creeps," snarled Rabid Rebecca. "Or I'll give you something to scream about."

"We saw . . . we saw . . ." gasped Ralph.

"A headless ghost," gasped Henry. "Outside the window."

Rabid Rebecca snorted.

"Yeah, right," she said. "Now shut up and go to sleep."

She left, slamming the door behind
her.

"Go!" said Horrid Henry.

Horrid Henry ran into the kitchen,
panting and gasping.

There were the bogey babysitters,
huddled over the cake. One slice was
already gone.

Rabid Rebecca looked up, cake knife
in hand.

"I smell a child," she hissed.

"What are you doing down here?" roared Rancid Rachel. "Go away before we . . ."

"I'm scared," said Horrid Henry. "I heard a noise."

"You're just trying to make an excuse to get out of bed, you little worm," said Rebecca.

"You'd better get out of here before I count to three," bellowed Rachel. "Or else."

"There's something outside," said Henry. "One

Two

Thr—"

Clink.

Clink.

Clink.

The clinking noise was coming from

outside the kitchen window.

"There," whimpered Horrid Henry.
He backed away.

"What was that?" said Rebecca, the
cake halfway to her drooling jaws.

"Nothing," said Rachel, shoving a
huge bit in her mouth.

Clink.
Clink.
Clink.

Rachel stopped chewing.

"That," hissed Rabid Rebecca. "That
clinking noise."

"I told you there's something
outside," whispered Horrid Henry.

Bang.
Bang.
Bang.

Rancid Rachel stood up.

"Ahh, it's just the wind," she said.

Bang.
Bang.
Bang.

"I'll show you," said Rachel. "I'm not scared."

She marched over to the window and drew back the curtain.

There in the dark was a headless suit, flapping and rapping at the window.

"AAARRRGGGHHH!" screeched Rebecca. She spat out her mouthful.

"AAARRRGGHHHH!" screeched Rachel. She spat out her mouthful.

"It's a ghost! Hide!" they howled,

racing from the kitchen and clambering
up the stairs.

"Go outside and see what it is,"
screamed Horrid Henry.

"No way," shrieked
Rebecca.

They barricaded
themselves into the
bathroom and locked
the door.

Horrid Henry snatched
the cake off the cake stand
and raced back to Ralph's
room.

Ralph was standing at the
open window, dangling a
hanger from a string with
his dad's suit on it.

Henry beamed at
Ralph as he hauled in the
suit and untied the keys

he'd used to clink on the ground.

Ralph beamed at Henry.

"Good job, partner," said Henry, helping himself to a gigantic piece of chocolate cake. Hmmm boy, it was delicious.

"Good job, partner," said Ralph, digging into an even bigger one.

"Won't your mum be furious with Rebecca when she comes home and finds all the cake gone?" mumbled Henry, taking another enormous slice.

"Boy will she ever," said Ralph. "I bet Rebecca never babysits here again."

2

....

HORRID HENRY TELLS IT LIKE IT IS

Why, asked Horrid Henry, was he uniquely cursed? Why, of all the homework in the world, did he have to make a five minute movie about his gag–blecccch–yuck family instead of a thrilling film about mutant zombies or werewolf teachers?

Ugghh. His family were *so* boring. Horrid Henry yawned just thinking about them.

He was a famous film director. He'd made the soon-to-be Hollywood classic, *The Undead Demon Monster Who*

Would Not Die. And the sequel – *The Revenge Of The Undead Demon Monster Who Would Not Die.* Part 3 would be coming soon – *The Undead Demon Monster Who Would Not Die – This Time It's Personal!!!* He was an artist. A genius. How dare Miss Battle-Axe tell a filmmaker like him what kind of movie to make? When he moved to Hollywood, he'd have Miss Battle-Axe

play a corpse in every film he made. *And* do all her own stunts. Falling out of a skyscraper. Tightrope walking between two buildings. Being caught in an avalanche.

AAAARRGGHH!

Why couldn't he just make the film he wanted? He liked films about monsters. And ghosts. And aliens.

27

But
no. Their
topic was
All About
My Family
and that's what
he had to do.

Naturally he'd left it to the last
minute.

"I need to borrow your camera,"
said Henry after a revolting supper of
Vegetable Bake with extra Brussels
sprouts and fruit for − ha ha − "dessert".

28

"I have to ask you questions about our family and film you. It's homework." He scowled.

Mum stopped stacking dirty plates.

"When's it due?" said Mum.

Henry had hoped she wouldn't ask that.

"Ummm . . . let me see . . . tomorrow," said Henry.

"Why do you always leave everything to the last minute?" said Dad.

Wasn't it obvious? Who wanted to do boring homework when there were so many comics to read and so much good telly to watch and so many packs of crisps to eat? His parents were dummies.

"*I* don't leave anything to the last minute," said Perfect Peter. "I always do *my* homework the moment I get home from school."

29

Mum smiled at him. "Quite right, Peter."

"Shut up, Peter," said Henry.

"Mum, Henry told me to shut up," said Peter.

"Don't tell your brother to shut up," said Mum.

"I wouldn't have to if he wasn't so ANNOYING," said Henry.

"I'm not annoying, Henry's annoying," said Peter.

Horrid Henry laughed.

"Why are you laughing?" said Peter.

"I'm laughing at your wibble wobble pants," said Henry.

Peter looked down at his trousers.

"I don't have wibble wobble pants," said Peter.

"Do too."

"Do not."

"Do too Nappy Noodle Wibble

Wobble Pants."

"Mum!" screamed Peter. "Henry called me a Nappy Noodle AND a Wibble Wobble Pants."

"Don't be horrid, Henry," shouted Mum. "Or no filming."

"But it's for homework!" shrieked Henry.

"Can we get on with this?" said Dad. "I'm very busy."

"All right," said Henry. "I'll be quick." Boy would he ever. Just a

31

few minutes and everyone's misery –
especially his – would be over.

"Do a sound check first," said Dad.
"Make sure it's loud enough and
recording."

"Okay," said Henry. He pointed the
camera and switched it on.

"Say Disgusting. Horrible. Yuck." said
Henry.

"Disgusting. Horrible. Yuck." said
Dad.

Henry pressed Replay.

"Disgusting. Horrible. Yuck." came
Dad's voice, loud and clear.

"This film is called ALL ABOUT MY
FAMILY," said Henry, pointing the
camera at Dad.

Now, what to ask, what to ask?
thought Henry.

Fat Fluffy started snoring in the
corner.

"Dad, how would you describe our cat Fluffy?"

Dad paused.

"A big fatty," said Dad. "To be honest, she really needs to lose weight. Why does she eat so much? Every time I see her she's chomping away."

"Sound check, Mum," said Henry. "Smelly. Revolting. Ick."

"Smelly. Revolting. Ick." said Mum.

Henry pointed the camera at his mother wiping the table.

"Mum, say three adjectives that describe you," said Henry.

33

"Oh, uhhm, hard-working, kind, thoughtful," said Mum.

I'd say mean, bossy and grumpy, thought Horrid Henry. Too bad *he* wasn't answering the questions.

"Who's your favourite child, Mum?"

"Henry!" snapped Mum. "Don't be horrid."

"All right," said Henry, scowling. He was only trying to make things a bit more fun.

"What's your favourite undead monster?"

"Afraid I don't have one," said Mum.

Why did he have such boring parents? How could someone *not* have a favourite undead monster? thought Henry.

"Dad, who is your eldest son?"

"Henry."

"Who is your youngest son?"

"Peter," said Mum, smiling.

"Definitely Peter," said Dad.

Henry swivelled the camera to Peter. Peter beamed and waved.

"Hello," said Peter. "Do you want to see my Bunnikins?"

"No," said Henry.

"When are you going to interview me?" said Peter. "I'm in your family."

"Worse luck," muttered Henry. "Now Worm, to check the sound, can you say Wibble Wobble Poopy Pants?"

"I don't want to say Wibble Wobble Poopy Pants!" screamed Peter.

"Don't be horrid, Henry," said Dad. "I don't want to hear any more

Wibble Wobble Poopy Pants from you."

"OK, OK," said Horrid Henry. "Say Fantastic. Marvellous. The best."

"Fantastic. Marvellous. The best." said Peter.

"What's your name?" Henry was practically falling asleep.

"Peter," said Peter.

"Who's your favourite teacher?"

"Miss Lovely."

"Tell me about your wonderful brother Henry," said Henry.

Peter paused.

"Henry is my big brother," said Peter. "He's mean to me."

"Peter!" said Mum.

"Well, he is. And I want everyone to know."

"And you're a worm," said Henry.

"Mum!" wailed Peter.

"What do you think about my teacher, Miss Battle-Axe?" said Henry, pointing the camera at Dad.

"She's brilliant," said Dad.

"Mum!" wailed Peter again. "Henry called me a worm."

"What do you think about Miss Lovely?" said Henry.

"The best teacher in the school," said Dad.

Blah blah blah. That was surely enough. Horrid Henry switched off the camera.

"That's . . . uhh . . . great," said Henry. Not.

Horrid Henry sat on his bed and played back his film. It was even more boring than he'd feared. His reputation as a great filmmaker would be ruined.

Wasn't there any way he could make

it more interesting? More fun? More unique?

Then Horrid Henry watched the film again. And again. Hmmm. Hmmm.

What about if he . . . jiggled things around a bit? After all, wasn't editing what set a film director apart from the crowd?

Henry sat down at his computer and went to work. A little snip here, a little trim there . . .

"Right, everyone face front," barked Miss Battle-Axe.

"Graham! Put those crisps away.

Ralph! Stop burping.

Meg! Stop shouting."

Graham kept eating. Ralph kept burping. Megaphone Meg kept shouting.

Miss Battle-Axe mopped her brow. One day she would wake up and this would all be a bad dream and she would be doing her real job tap dancing on Broadway.

"We're going to watch your All About My Family films," she said.

"Mine!" shrieked Megaphone Meg.

"Mine! shrieked Fiery Fiona.

"Mine!" shrieked Zippy Zoe.

"I'll start with someone who is sitting beautifully."

Miss Battle-Axe peered round the class. The only person sitting beautifully was Moody Margaret who was pretending she hadn't just pulled Sour Susan's hair when Miss Battle-Axe wasn't looking.

Miss Battle-Axe pressed Play.

There was Margaret, looking like a hideous frog as usual. She was wearing lipstick and a big bow in her hair.

"All About My Family," said Moody

Margaret. "But naturally, this film is about the most interesting and important person in my family, me."

The camera swivelled.

"So Mum," said Margaret, "Everyone wants to know, why am I the most amazing person who has ever lived in the history of the world?"

"Ooh, Maggie Moo Moo," said Margaret's mum, "I'm not sure five minutes is long enough to list all your wonderful qualities."

Horrid Henry mooed under his breath.

"That's right, Maggie Plumpykins," said her dad. "We couldn't begin—"

"Obviously not, but hurry up and start," snapped Margaret, turning the camera back on herself.

"You're the most beautiful, talented, clever, amazing, brilliant, remarkable, extra—"

43

Rude Ralph belched.

"Don't be rude, Ralph," said Miss Battle-Axe.

Henry made a vomiting noise.

"Blecccchhhhh."

"Henry! I'm warning you."

Blah Blah Blah. Five long horrible minutes of Margaret's parents bragging about her. It felt like five years.

Yawn. When would they get to the star of the day?

"Now Margaret, you can choose whose film we watch next," said Miss Battle-Axe.

Sour Susan smirked.

Margaret swept her eyes over the class.

"William's," she said.

Miss Battle-Axe pressed Play.

There was a shot of a white ceiling. Then the film zoomed down to a pair of feet. There was a bit of mumbling in the background.

Then the sound of weeping.

"Wah!" wailed Weepy William. He burst into tears. "I did it wrong."

Bert's film was next.

"I dunno," said Bert's mum.

"I dunno," said Bert's dad.

"I dunno," said Beefy Bert's brother.

Miss Battle-Axe frowned.

Horrid Henry waved his hand frantically.

"All right, Henry," said Miss Battle-Axe. She pressed Play.

The film opened in the kitchen. Mum, Dad and Peter were sitting smiling at the messy table.

"Dad, how would you describe *Mrs Oddbod*?" came Henry's voice off-camera.

"A big fatty," said Dad. "To be honest, she really needs to lose weight. Why does she eat so much? Every time I see her she's chomping away."

"Mum, say three adjectives that describe *me*."

"Oh, hard-working, kind, thoughtful," said Mum, beaming.

"Mum, say three adjectives that describe *Peter*."

"Smelly. Revolting. Ick." said Mum.

"What's your favourite undead monster?"

"Peter," said Mum.

"Who's your favourite child, Mum?"

"Henry!" shouted Mum.

"Who is your *best* son?" asked Henry.

"Henry," said Dad.

"Who is the most horrible person you know?"

"Peter," said Mum smiling.

"Definitely Peter," said Dad.

The camera switched to Peter.

Peter smiled and waved.

"Hello," said Peter. "Do you want to see my Bunnikins?"

"No," said Henry.

"When are you going to interview me?" said Peter. "I'm in your family."

"What's your name?" came Henry's voice-over.

"Wibble Wobble Poopy Pants," yelled Peter.

"Who's your *worst* teacher?"

48

"Miss Lovely."

"Tell me about your wonderful brother Henry," said Henry.

"Henry is my big brother. He's . . . fantastic. Marvellous. The best."

"Peter!" said Mum.

"Well, he is. I want everyone to know," said Peter.

"What do you think about my teacher Miss Battle-Axe?"

"Smelly. Revolting. Ick." said Mum.

"What do you think about Miss Lovely?"

"Wibble Wobble Poopy Pants," said Dad.

"Well," said Mrs Oddbod, switching off her computer.

Mum, Dad and Henry sat in her office. Mum and Dad looked like they

49

wished a magic carpet would fly in and whisk them off to a faraway planet.

"Henry, how could you?" said Mum.

"We're shocked," said Dad.

"We're appalled," said Mum.

Horrid Henry scowled.

Honestly.

Was this the thanks he got for trying hard at homework for once?

Geniuses are never recognised in their lifetime, thought Horrid Henry sadly.

3

HORRID HENRY'S KRAZY KETCHUP

"Boys," shouted Mum up the stairs. "Dinner's ready."

"Ralph! Catch."

Horrid Henry threw Fluff Puff, Peter's favourite plastic sheep, to Ralph.

Rude Ralph caught it, and threw it back to Henry over Peter's head.

"Give me back my sheep," said Perfect Peter.

"How much will you pay me, Wormy Worm?" said Horrid Henry.

"Mum!" screamed Perfect Peter.

"Henry stole Fluff Puff and he won't give him back. And he called me Wormy Worm."

"Tell-tale," hissed Henry.

Fluff Puff flew through the air, a sheep in flight, and landed smack on the floor.

"Henry," shouted Mum. "Say sorry for calling Peter names. And get down here NOW."

"Sorry I called you Wormy Worm," said Henry, "when I meant to call you

Poopsicle."

"MUUUUM!"
shrieked Peter.
He picked up
Fluff Puff and ran
downstairs.

"Boys. For the last
time. Dinner's ready."

Henry and Ralph stomped downstairs
and sat at the table.

"What's for dinner?" said Horrid
Henry.

"Cauliflower cheese," said Dad.

"Ick," said Henry.

"Yuck," said Ralph, rudely. "I hate
cauliflower. I need ketchup."

"Yeah," said Horrid Henry. "Me too.
Ketchup makes everything taste great."

"No ketchup for me," said Perfect
Peter. "It's much too sweet."

Mum smiled at Peter.

"It certainly is," said Mum. "Ketchup has lots of sugar in it."

Wow, thought Horrid Henry. Wow. Ketchup was even more wonderful than he'd thought. When he became a billionaire with his top secret ketchup recipes, and, naturally, his own brand, *Henry's Incredible Ketchup*, he'd put in loads more sugar. Then it would taste even better.

Mum
reached for
the sauce and
squirted a
teeny weeny
drop onto
Henry's plate. Then she did the same to
Ralph's plate.

"That's not enough," Henry howled.
"I need MORE. I want ketchup on my
ketchup."

"Yeah," said Rude Ralph. "Gimme
more."

How could anyone eat cauliflower
unless its horrible white knobbly-ness
was covered in ketchup? And beans
without ketchup? Or eggs without
ketchup? Gross. Nothing could hide
their horrible beaniness, or revolting
egginess, but ketchup helped.

"Don't be horrid, Henry," said Mum.

57

"But I LOVE ketchup," said Horrid Henry. He loved the taste of ketchup. He loved the smell of ketchup. He loved the glug glug glug noise ketchup made as it slurped out of the bottle and plopped onto his plate. There was nothing that didn't taste a million billion trillion times better covered in yummy scrummy Krazy Ketchup, the world's best brand.

Every hundred years or so, when his mean, horrible parents took  him to Brilliant Burger, he'd snatch loads of their Krazy Ketchup sachets to stash in his bedroom, just in case the world ended or all the ketchup factories burned down.

Yum. Yum. Yummm. Krazy Ketchup. The nicest two words in the English language. (Apart from *chocolate*, *pizza*, *burger*, *chips*, *Make Your Own Hot Fudge Sundae*, and *No School Today*.)

Unfortunately, Horrid Henry's parents hated ketchup. They hated the taste of ketchup. They hated the smell of ketchup. Most of all, they hated it when Henry wanted ketchup at every meal.

But how else could he eat his parents'

disgusting food? One day Mum and
Dad would find his skeleton in a corner,
bony hands

outstretched
towards the
fridge . . .
Didn't they
know you
could *die*
from lack of
ketchup?

"My family eat *everything* with
ketchup," said Ralph. "Pasta with
ketchup, mashed potatoes with
ketchup, ice cream with ketchup. And I
always squirt my own. I'm not a baby."

"See?" said Henry.

Mum made a face.

"Everyone I know gets to squirt their
own ketchup," wailed Horrid Henry.
"Everyone except *me*. I wish Ralph's

parents were mine instead of *you*."

Mum looked at Dad.

Dad looked at Mum.

"No one *I* know squirts their own," said Perfect Peter. "Little children always take too much."

Horrid Henry kicked Peter under the table.

"Mum!" squealed Peter. "Henry kicked me."

"Didn't."

"Did."

"It was an accident," said Horrid Henry. "I was just stretching my legs. I can't help it if *yours* got in the way."

"What's for dessert?" said Ralph rudely, pushing away his plate.

"Fruit salad," said Mum.

"Blecccch," said Rude Ralph. "I'm not eating dinner *here* again."

Horrid Henry lay on his bed reading a Mutant Max comic and scoffing a few biscuits from his top secret tin.

Knock Knock.

Henry leapt up and ran to his desk.
"I'm doing my homework," he said.
Mum and Dad peeped round the door.
"Maybe we've been too strict," said Mum.
What? thought Henry.
"We'll try it tomorrow and see," said Dad.
"Try what?" said Horrid Henry, scowling. Some yucky new food? Making him do even more chores? Living without TV?

"Try letting you squirt your own ketchup," said Mum.

Henry's jaw dropped. Was it possible that his parents had actually *listened?* That for once in his life he was getting his own way? Had aliens taken over their bodies?

But Horrid Henry wasn't going to ruin everything by asking.

Ketchup Ketchup Ketchup here I come! he crowed. Oh happy happy day.

Sniff. Sniff. Sniff.

Horrid Henry stopped turning all of Peter's sheep upside down.

What was that yummy smell? Henry sniffed again.

Chips! thought Horrid Henry. He could smell their lovely frying golden goodness all the way upstairs.

They were actually having chips with dinner. On the first day that the new squirt-your-own-ketchup rules applied. What luck.

For once his chips would be swimming in a ketchup bath. Oh yeah. And he'd be sure to steal loads of Peter's when he wasn't looking. Tee hee.

Horrid Henry dropped Fluff Puff on his head and galloped down the stairs.

Oh wow. Even better. Fish fingers *and* chips!

Unfortunately, Dad was sure to ruin everything and make peas too, but he could disguise their hideous green taste by drowning them in yummy, scrummy ketchup.

Speaking of which–

Horrid Henry looked in the fridge.

No ketchup.
He flung open
the cupboard.
No ketchup.
He checked on
the table, behind
the toaster, and
on top of the counter.

Had Mum
hidden it? Had
Dad secretly
guzzled it?

Had the thing
Horrid Henry
dreaded most
in all the world
actually happened?

Henry's blood ran cold. His heart
stopped beating. His nose stopped
breathing. His legs collapsed under him.

"Where's the ketchup?" gasped

Horrid Henry. "I'll starve without it. How could we run out of ketchup? You said I could pour my own and now there's no ketchup to pour. NOOOOOOOO!"

"Stop being horrid, Henry," said Mum. "It's on the table."

"Right in front of your nose," said Dad, opening the oven and taking out the fish fingers and chips.

Horrid Henry stopped howling and sat down in his chair.

A brown plastic bottle with a big picture of a smiling speckled tomato stood on the table.

"What's *that*?" said Henry suspiciously.

"Ketchup," said Mum.

"No it isn't," said Henry.

"It's just as tasty," said Dad.

Horrid Henry squinted at the bottle. *Vegchup Tomato Ketchup* read the label.

Horrid Henry recoiled as if a poisonous hydra had just reared its nine heads.

"Ick!" said Henry. He made a gagging noise. "This has *tomatoes* in it. I want real ketchup. I want Krazy Ketchup."

"All ketchup has tomatoes in it," said Mum.

"No way," said Horrid Henry.

He hated tomatoes. He knew it was called *tomato* ketchup but he'd just thought it was referring to ketchup being red. Not that there were actual, real *tomatoes* in it.

"Go ahead, try some," said Mum, serving up the chips. "You can pour your own."

Horrid Henry squirted a great big fat blob onto his pirate plate.

It wasn't a lovely, thick, red ketchuppy blob. This blob was brown. Watery. Oily. It oozed on the plate.

"It looks horrible," screamed Henry.

"How can you tell until you try it?" said Mum.

Horrid Henry screwed up his face and took a teeny tiny taste.

Blecccccchhhh.

He spat it out.

"It's HORRIBLE!!! I can taste the tomatoes. And vegetables!"

"This is organic, healthy, sugar free ketchup," said Mum.

"Sounds yummy," said Perfect Peter.

"I can't wait to try some."

"Shut up Peter," said Henry.

"Mum," wailed Peter. "Henry told me to shut up."

"I want Krazy Ketchup!" screamed Horrid Henry. "Gimme real ketchup."

"This is real ketchup," said Peter. He reached for the bottle.

"No it isn't," shouted Henry. "Does this look like ketchup to you?"

Horrid Henry snatched the bottle from Peter.

Peter tried to yank it back.

"Henry! Peter! Stop fighting!" screamed Mum, grabbing the bottle.

"Gimme that ketchup," said Dad.

Squeeze!
Splat!
Plop!
Glop!

Ketchup landed on Mum's head. Ketchup landed on Dad's face. Ketchup splatted on Peter's jumper and Henry's shirt.

There was ketchup on the floor. There was ketchup on the door. There was ketchup on the ceiling. Mum, Dad, Peter and Henry were covered in ketchup.

"EEEEKK," yelled Mum.

"Take your plates and go to your rooms, both of you!" yelled Dad.

"Wah," wailed Peter.

Ketchup dribbled down Mum's face. She licked her lips.

"This tastes horrible," she said.

Dad wiped some ketchup off his face and licked his finger.

He scowled.

"Ugh," he said. "That's revolting."

"See?" said Horrid Henry. "Told you."

Horrid Henry sat on his bed drowning his chips in sachet after sachet of his emergency Krazy Ketchup stash. He knew he'd been right to stockpile it.

Ah! Krazy Ketchup and chips. Was there anything better to eat in the whole wide world?

And oh yes. He had the feeling that Krazy Ketchup would be back in his kitchen *very* soon.

4

HORRID HENRY'S CHICKEN

Oh joy! Oh rapture! It was the last day of school before the Easter break. Henry had been counting down the weeks. Then the days. The hours. The minutes. No more school. No more Miss Battle-Axe. No more homework. Hello telly. Hello crisps. Hello pyjamas all day.

And hello April Fool's day soon. Henry had great plans. Salt in the sugar bowl. Moving all the clocks forward. Mixing shampoo with grass and making Peter think Fat Fluffy had thrown up.

A few pop-pop snapper-
crackers on the loo seat.
Hanging Peter's underpants
on his overhead light.
   Yippee!
   Nothing could spoil
his happiness. Nothing.
Nothing. Nothing. Not even
if Mum insisted he play with
Peter every single day. Not
even if—

76

Squawk.
Squawk.
Squawk.

Horrid Henry scowled. And then he beamed. The holidays meant he wouldn't have to hear that horrible chicken cackle for two whole weeks.

AAAAARRRGGHHH! Why couldn't his class have a rabbit, or a guinea pig, or a goldfish as a class pet? Instead, they had a chicken. Not just any chicken. A horrible chicken. A huge, horrible, *EVIL* chicken. Her name was Dolores. Ugh. Henry trembled just thinking about her mean chickeny eyes and her pointy chickeny feet and her fiery chickeny breath.

Horrid Henry was afraid of nothing (except injections). The biggest snake? Phooey. The hairiest spider? Bah. But

77

Horrid Henry was terrified of – shhhh – chickens.

This was Henry's deepest, darkest secret. Who's scared of a chicken? Who was so *chicken* they were scared of a chicken? Even Anxious Andrew happily fed Dolores.

But Horrid Henry was sure Dolores was out to get him. Whenever he walked past her coop she glared. Henry had nightmares about her chasing him with her jabbing stabbing peck peck pecking beak.

EEEEEEK!

Henry shuddered and poked Ralph.

"I dare you to burp," whispered Henry.

"Stop burping, Ralph!" snapped Miss Battle-Axe.

"I have an important announcement," she added, fixing them with her Medusa glare, "Sad as I know you all are not to be in school for *such* a long time . . ."

As if, thought Horrid Henry.

"I'm happy to tell you that one lucky person will be having Dolores for the holidays."

"I want her," screamed Moody Margaret.

"I want her," screamed Inky Ian.

"I want her," drooled Greedy Graham.

"Ugg," grunted Stone-Age Steven.

"This wouldn't happen in Norway," said Norwegian Norris.

"Silence!" roared Miss Battle-Axe. "I've put all your names into a hat, and the winner gets Dolores."

Horrid Henry picked up his pencil

and started drawing
a monster dangling
Miss Battle-Axe
from its acid-dripping
mouth all over his
spelling test. Phew. He

was safe. He never won anything. Who
knew being unlucky would pay off one
day?

Miss Battle-Axe reached into the hat.

"And the lucky person having Dolores
is . . ." said Miss Battle-Axe, peering at
the slip of paper, ". . . Henry!"

"Wah," wailed Weepy William.

"What?" said Henry. He stopped
drawing daggers. What was she telling
him off for *now*?

"You've got Dolores," said Miss
Battle-Axe.

He . . . *what*?

He had . . . Dolores? Deadly Dolores?

81

The foulest fowl on the planet? That monster in feathers? That demented demon?

Horrid Henry opened his mouth to scream, NOOOOOO! I DON'T WANT HER!!!!!!!

Then he shut his mouth. What if someone suspected his terrible secret? That he, Horrid Henry, the terror of teachers, the squisher of sitters, the fearless leader of a pirate gang, was scared of – a chicken. He'd never hear the end of the teasing and squawking.

Dolores glared at Henry.

Henry glared at Dolores.

Was it his imagination, or was she already sharpening her beak?

Henry gulped.

Actually, why was he worried? His mean horrible parents would *never* let

him have a chicken. He'd bring her
home, and then Mum would make
him take her straight back to school.
Sorted.

"What fun, a chicken," said Mum.

"Yum, yum, think of all the fresh eggs
we'll be having," said Dad.

"Henry, I expect you to take good
care of her," said Mum. "That means
cleaning out her box and letting her
roam in the garden during the day as
well as feeding her."

Horrid Henry could scarcely breathe.
Was Mum insane? He could just about
cope with throwing some corn at
Dolores from a safe distance. But Mum
wanted him to . . . to . . . clean up
chicken poo? Dolores would be lying
in wait for him. His last moments on
earth — covered in chicken poo while

a marauding chicken ripped him limb
from limb.

AAAARRRRGGGHHHH!

Horrid Henry avoided Deadly Dolores
for as long as he could.

"No pocket money and no TV until
you take care of that chicken," said
Dad.

"Later," said Henry. His heart was
pounding.

"Right now," said Mum.

"No more excuses," said Dad.

"I always clean out Fluffy's litter box without being asked," said Perfect Peter.

"Then why don't you sleep in it, you poopy pants worm," said Henry.

"Mum," wailed Peter. "Henry called me a poopy pants worm."

"Stop being horrid, Henry, and clean out that chicken," said Mum.

"The eggs will go rotten if you don't collect them," said Dad.

"Eggs! Eggs! Eggs!" said Peter. "We want eggs."

Eggs?! Who cared about eggs? While they were all fussing about eggs he'd be pecked to death by Dracula Chicken.

"OKAY," screamed Horrid Henry. Serve them right when they went looking for him and all that was left was a shoe and some bones.

Blood-sucking, cackling chicken, muttered Henry. Bet she really did belong to Dracula. Bet her *real* name was Cackula.

Slowly, he walked towards the little red hen house at the end of the garden, carrying fresh straw, some old newspaper and a rake. Ugh. Bleccch. Gross. Clean out the hen house? *Clean* out the hen house?! He, Henry, have to touch . . . chicken poo? NOOOOOOOO!

Henry was sure Cackula did it on purpose. Surely no normal chicken

could make such a mess? She did it
to lure him closer. The moment he
touched her straw, he knew she'd
charge at him, wielding her terrifying
beak and scratching claws. Cackula
didn't eat corn and grubs. Cackula ate –
Henrys!

Horrid Henry peeked in through the
chicken wire. Maybe he could take her
by surprise, he thought.

But no. There she was, lying in wait,
her evil eyes glinting.

Horrid Henry trembled and stepped
back.

Then he squared his shoulders. What
was he, a man or a . . . a . . . *chicken*?

Chicken, he squeaked.

I will not be defeated by a chicken
named Dolores, he thought.

He opened the hen house door the
teensiest weensiest bit.

Squawk! Squawk! Squawk!

A stinky, smelly blast hit him in the face as Deadly Dolores reared off her perch.

Henry slammed the hen house door shut. He stood there, gasping and

panting. Wow. What a lucky escape from death by chicken.

He might not be so fortunate next time.

There was NO way he was going near that murderous beast.

But what to do, what to do? He could hardly admit he was – gulp – scared of a chicken. And even if by some miracle he survived, who wanted to spend their precious holidays clearing up chicken poo?

When he was king, all chickens would be banned unless they were wrapped in cellophane or coated in breadcrumbs.

His holiday was ruined.

"Here, chick chick chick," cooed a little voice behind him. "I've got a lovely treat for you."

"Pwooah Pwooah Pwooah," went Dolores, pretending to be a sweet, friendly fowl.

"Peter's here, you lovely fluffy little chicken," cheeped Peter. "Can I collect the eggs, Henry?"

"No," said Henry automatically.

"Please?"

"NO!"

"Why?" said Peter.

Suddenly Henry froze. What if . . . what if . . . what if he could get *Peter* to do his dirty work for him? That would be the best, the greatest trick ever in the history of the world. No, the universe!

Henry beckoned Peter closer and whispered in his ear.

"I can't let you because they're *magic* eggs. But if you tell *anyone* you'll be mashed to smithereens," said Henry.

"What do you mean, they're magic eggs?" said Peter.

"Keep your voice down," hissed Henry. "Just what I said. So no way are you going near my magic chicken."

"How do you know she's magic?" said Peter.

"You've read Jack and the Beanstalk haven't you?" said Henry. "Well, Dolores is related to that chicken. Except *she* lays chocolate eggs."

"*Chocolate* eggs?" said Peter. "How can she lay chocolate eggs?"

Henry shrugged. "How can she lay *eggie* eggs? She's not the only magic chicken in the world, you know. Where do you think all the chocolate eggs come from? But because I'm such a nice brother, I'll share the eggs with you."

"You will?" said Peter.

"But on one condition. You clean out the hen house, you get to keep the eggs."

"*All* the chocolate eggs?" said Peter. "Every single one?"

"Yup," said Henry.

"Okay," said Peter.

Tee hee, thought Henry. What a worm his brother was. Tricking him was so much fun. Really, he should do it more often.

Peter approached the hen box and reached inside. Henry, naturally, had an answer ready for when Peter found it empty.

"Duh, of course there aren't any magic eggs *yet*," he'd say. "You have to *clean* out her nest first. She's not going to lay a chocolate egg in a poo house, is she?"

That way, he'd get Peter to muck out the hen house for the *entire* holiday, hoping to get magic eggs. Ha! Sorted. He was a genius. His plan was perfect. No more poo. No more Dolores. TV here I come, thought Horrid Henry.

Perfect Peter squealed.

"Look what I've found," said Peter. He held out his hand. "There's loads and loads and loads of them."

Perfect Peter was holding a chocolate egg.

Huh?

What?

How could this be? Could there really be . . .

Horrid Henry forgot he was scared of chickens.

Horrid Henry forgot Cackula was out to get him.

Horrid Henry shoved Peter aside and pushed the squawking Dolores off her nest.

There in the straw was a huge, glistening pile of gleaming chocolate eggs.

"Come get us, Henry," cooed the eggs.

"Out of my way, Worm!" shrieked Henry.

"But you said—" shrieked Peter.

"That was then," screamed Henry, shoving Peter out of the way. "They're all mine."

"Mine!" screamed Peter.

"Mine!" screamed Henry.

"Gimme those eggs or the giant will get you," said Henry.

"What giant?" said Peter.

"I told you. Dolores belongs to the giant in Jack and the Beanstalk. He'll be coming for her . . . and then for YOU!"

"I don't think so," said Peter. He backed away, holding onto his egg. "And do you know why?"

"NO," snarled Horrid Henry, blocking Peter and snatching chocolate eggs from the nest as fast as he could. He felt like dancing for joy. He had a magic chicken. He'd find a way to keep Dolores. He'd tell Miss Battle-Axe they'd eaten her for Sunday lunch by mistake. Then he'd have chocolate forever. Horrid Henry hugged himself. He could set up a shop – Henry's

Amazing Chocolate Eggs. People would come for miles to buy his chocolate and peek at his magic, chocolate-egg-laying chicken. He'd charge them £100 just to *look* at Dolores.

He'd be rich, rich, rich!

"April Fool!" shouted Peter.

"April Fool!" shouted Mum.

"April Fool!" shouted Dad.

"Squawk!" cackled Dolores, ruffling her feathers.

Oh. Oh no.

Horrid Henry had been so anxious about Dolores he'd completely forgotten about April Fool's day.

"We thought you'd NEVER find them," said Mum.

"What took you so long?" said Dad.

"I tricked you, Henry," said Perfect Peter. He couldn't believe it. For once, *he'd* played a trick.

Horrid Henry stood still. His mind whirred.

But Horrid Henry was not the fearless leader of a pirate gang for nothing.

"In your dreams, Worm," said Horrid Henry, stuffing a chocolate egg in his mouth. "I was just *pretending* to believe you."

He patted Dolores on the head. She wasn't magic, but she wasn't a monster. Why on earth had he ever been scared of her?

He'd deal with Peter later. No one tried to trick Horrid Henry and lived to tell the tale.

Screams came from Peter's bedroom. Henry threw down his comic and ran to see.

There was Peter, covered in gooey

raw egg and holding a chocolate-covered shell. Goop dribbled down his chin and shirt and splattered onto his shoes.

"AAAARRRGGHHH!" squealed Peter.

"April Fool!" shrieked Horrid Henry.

Collect all the
Horrid Henry storybooks!

Horrid Henry

Horrid Henry
and the Secret Club

Horrid Henry Tricks
the Tooth Fairy

Horrid Henry
Gets Rich Quick

Horrid Henry's Nits

Horrid Henry's
Haunted House

Horrid Henry and
the Mummy's Curse

Horrid Henry's
Revenge

Horrid Henry and the
Bogey Babysitter

Horrid Henry's Stinkbomb

Horrid Henry's Underpants

the
orion star

★ ★ ★

CALLING ALL GROWN-UPS!

Sign up for **the orion star** newsletter to hear about your favourite authors and exclusive competitions, plus details of how children can join our 'Story Stars' review panel.

Sign up at:

www.orionbooks.co.uk/orionstar

Follow us 🐦 @the_orionstar

Find us ⓕ facebook.com/TheOrionStar